Rude Ramsay
~ AND THE ~
# Roaring Radishes

Margaret Atwood

Rude Ramsay
and the
Roaring
Radishes

ILLUSTRATED BY
Dušan Petričić

BLOOMSBURY
CHILDREN'S
BOOKS

Published by Bloomsbury, New York and London
Distributed to the trade by Holtzbrinck Publishers

Library of Congress Cataloging-in-Publication Data
Atwood, Margaret Eleanor.
  Rude Ramsay and the roaring radishes / Margaret Atwood ; illustrated by
  Dušan Petričić.
    p. cm.
  Summary: In this story told mainly with words that begin with the letter "r,"
  Rude Ramsay goes on an adventure with his friend Ralph the red-nosed rat.
  ISBN 1-58234-950-9 (alk. paper)
    [1. Behavior—Fiction. 2. Rats—Fiction. 3. Humorous stories.] I. Petričić,
    Dušan, ill. II. Title.
  PZ7.A895Ru 2004   [E]—dc22   2003065344

First U.S. Edition 2004
Previously published in Canada in 2003 by Key Porter Books Ltd.
Printed in Hong Kong/China
10 9 8 7 6 5 4 3 4 2 1

Bloomsbury USA Children's Books
175 Fifth Avenue
New York, NY 10010

For Madelaine and for R. and E. Cook, who will eat almost anything—M.A.

For my curious granddaughter Lara—D.P.

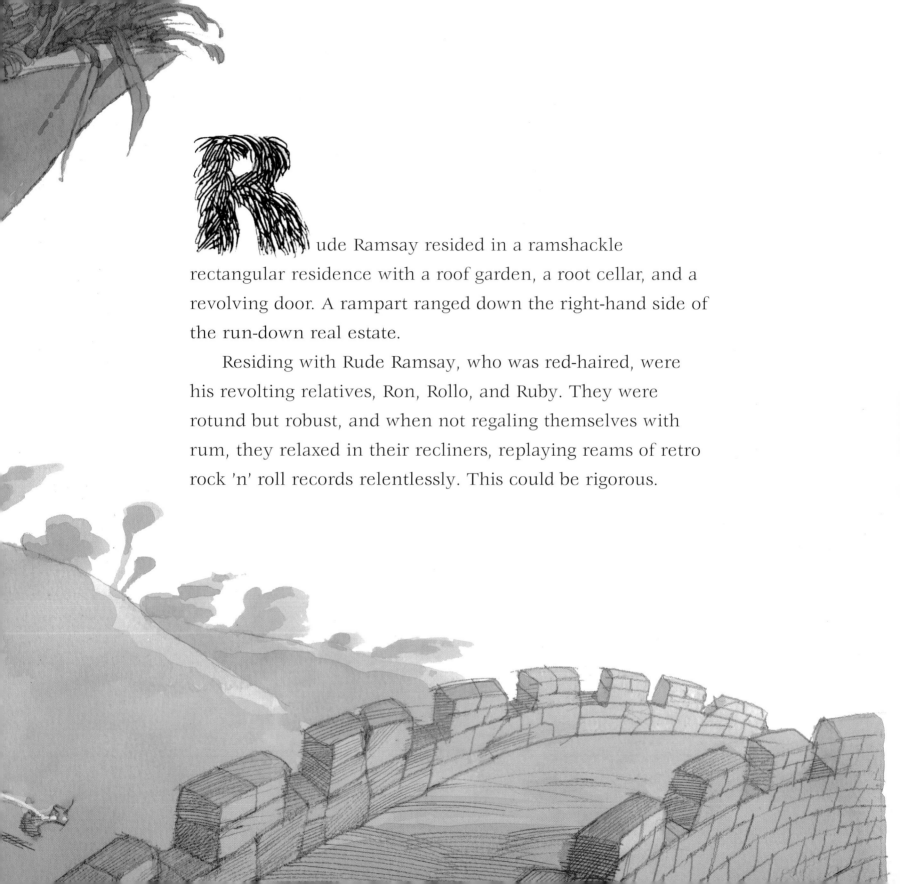

Rude Ramsay resided in a ramshackle rectangular residence with a roof garden, a root cellar, and a revolving door. A rampart ranged down the right-hand side of the run-down real estate.

Residing with Rude Ramsay, who was red-haired, were his revolting relatives, Ron, Rollo, and Ruby. They were rotund but robust, and when not regaling themselves with rum, they relaxed in their recliners, replaying reams of retro rock 'n' roll records relentlessly. This could be rigorous.

While Ron read the racing results, Ruby and Rollo regularly rustled up the repasts. They roasted rice, raisins, rutabagas, and rhinoceros. They rolled out reptiles with a rolling pin. They refrigerated rhubarb and broiled ribs, ravioli, and reindeer rinds on the rotisserie. The rice was rock-hard, the ribs rubbery, the ravioli wrinkled, the rhinoceros raw. The reptiles were still writhing, the rhubarb was runny, and the reindeer rinds were rotten.

Every Friday, Rude Ramsay rebelled. "This repast is repulsive," he'd report. "The rice is riddled with roaches, the raisins are rancid, and the reindeer rinds reek. I feel like regurgitating!"

"Ramsay, you rash, repulsive, red-headed runt! How rude! Rinse your mouth out with rope!" raged Ramsay's revolting relatives, Ron, Rollo, and Ruby. "Repent! Repent!"

"I refuse," retorted Ramsay.

Thoroughly riled, the three revolting relatives rose from the rejected repast and rushed after Ramsay, hurling ratchets, wrenches, wristwatches, rubber boots, and radios, which rebounded off Ramsay's rear. But Ramsay was a rapid runner, and he raced up to the roof garden and down to the root cellar and round and round the revolving door, until his robust but rotund relatives could no longer respire and required rest.

This ruckus was regarded by numerous raccoons, rabbits, robins, rollicking wrens, and rowdy, raggedy ravens, which were all roosting on the right-hand rampart, relishing the race and repeating raucously, "Rah! Rah!"

Ramsay's only friend was Ralph the red-nosed rat, a rubicund rodent. While Ramsay reclined upon a rumpled rucksack near the trash heap, rubbing his rust-colored bruises, Ralph rummaged among the roach-riddled rice and the rancid raisins and the remnants of reeking rhinoceros, remarking, "Rubbish is ravishing to rats. We revel in rotten reindeer rinds."

"Ripping for you," Ramsay retorted wretchedly. "You are a rat. But I'm ravenous. All this repeated running round and round is ruining me. I refer also to the retch-making recipes I am required to devour, and which I resent. I am less robust than my revolting relatives. I am receiving a raw deal. It rankles!"

"You might rove to the other side of the rampart," reflected one of the raggedy ravens. "Relocate your inner realm! Revive your rapport with nature! Refreshment awaits you there!"

"Be realistic," Ramsay replied. "The rampart is rough. It rises ridiculously high, and it is replete with rocks."

"I remember a round, Roman-vaulted rat-hole," remarked Ralph the red-nosed rat, while grooming his greasy whiskers. "It traverses the rampart, and might be wriggled through."

"Risky," retorted Rude Ramsay. "If rammed in rather far and unable to retreat, I will repine. Then, if it rains, I will drown. Rigor mortis will set in, as well as wrinkles. I am reluctant."

"Rise to the occasion," responded Ralph. "Resist restrictions! Be rugged!"

Together the pair resolved to dare the Roman-vaulted but risky rat-hole, which was crammed with rusty rivets, and assorted remnants, and the remains of rat nests, and was dripping with rivulets from the ragged rents in the rodent-riddled rampart. Ralph rocketed recklessly through, but Ramsay had to crawl, creeping over dark rubble and through narrow turnings, ripping his trousers on sharp rocks, wrecking his rubber-soled runners, and scraping his fingers. At last a rewarding ray of light pierced the remote end of the rat-hole.

Ramsay emerged into a resplendent realm. A ranch-sized garden with a river rippling through it revealed itself to his regard, rendering Ramsay rhapsodic. A rowboat rocked restfully. Roses enriched the redolent air with their aroma. Raspberry bushes ranged in reassuring rows.

Ramsay roamed among the raspberry rows, ripping off ripe raspberries and cramming them into his mouth. Ralph rambled restlessly, ransacking the region for root vegetables.

"Radishes! Radishes!" Ralph briskly reported.

"Right you are!" Ramsay responded. For there, around a corner, were rows and rows of round, red radishes, ready to be devoured. Surely they were organic! Ramsay hadn't relished a fresh radish ever since he could remember. What a rare treat!

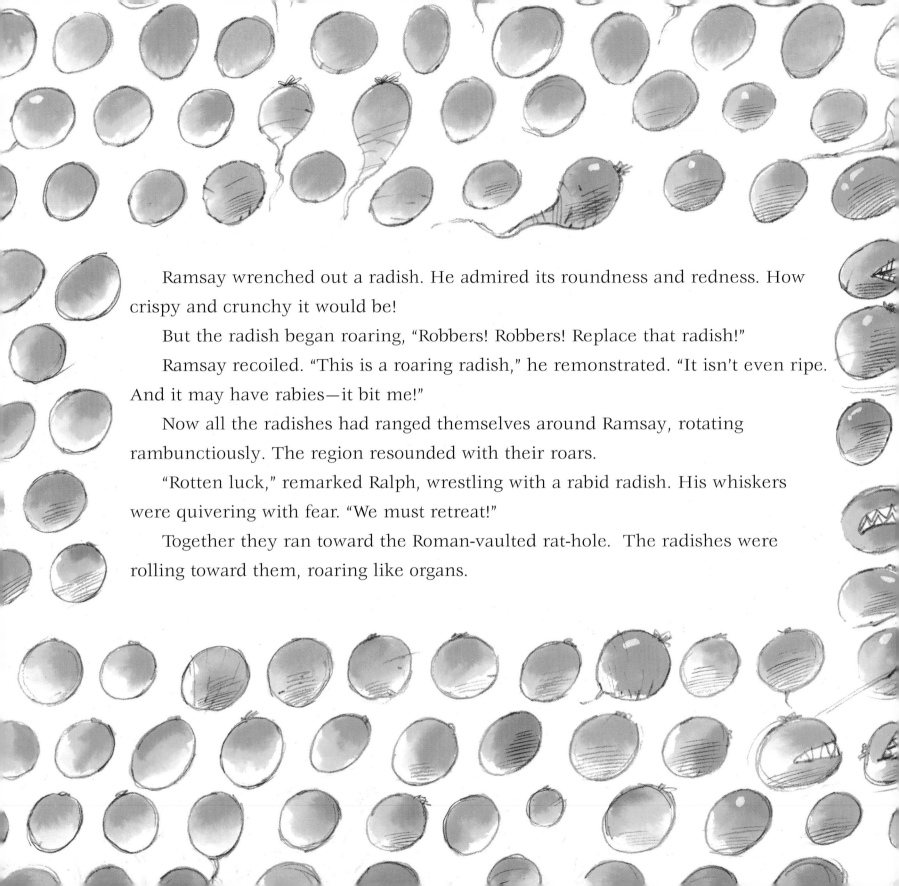

Ramsay wrenched out a radish. He admired its roundness and redness. How crispy and crunchy it would be!

But the radish began roaring, "Robbers! Robbers! Replace that radish!"

Ramsay recoiled. "This is a roaring radish," he remonstrated. "It isn't even ripe. And it may have rabies—it bit me!"

Now all the radishes had ranged themselves around Ramsay, rotating rambunctiously. The region resounded with their roars.

"Rotten luck," remarked Ralph, wrestling with a rabid radish. His whiskers were quivering with fear. "We must retreat!"

Together they ran toward the Roman-vaulted rat-hole. The radishes were rolling toward them, roaring like organs.

But then a small girl appeared. She had a red ruffled frock, raven ringlets with ribbons, and ribbed legwear. Over her arm she carried a receptacle for roses and raspberries.

"Why are you robbing me of my radishes?" she queried.

"What radishes?" replied Ramsay reticently. The radishes had now stopped roaring and were resolutely rerooting themselves in the ravaged radish rows.

"My name is Rillah," the small girl responded. "And you must be Rude Ramsay."

"You recognize me?" Ramsay was surprised.

"Only by remote reputation. I frequently hear your revolting relatives repeating that refrain. 'Rude Ramsay, you rash, repulsive, red-headed runt,' they rant. Would you like a rusk?" And she offered an assortment of rusks from her receptacle.

Ramsay and Ralph each reached for a rusk.

"Where do you reside?" Ralph inquired.

"In that romantic, recently restored rectory with the rotunda," replied Rillah.

Ramsay regarded the rectory. It was indeed romantic. Rhododendrons wreathed around it, fretwork trellises replete with trailing arbutus adorned it, a radiant rainbow arched above it.

"You must be royally rich," Ramsay remarked ruefully, remembering his own ramshackle residence. His trousers were ripped and his rubber-soled runners were wrecked. He resembled a ragamuffin. Surely Rillah would find him repellent. She would never be his friend. He wished she were a rat.

"Until recently I was rolling in rupees, but they have become rather scarce. My situation," reflected Rillah, "is the reverse of yours. You are rude, but at least you have relatives, however revolting. I am refined, but my relatives, although outwardly respectable and refulgently attired, are lacking in rectitude.

They rented a veritable regatta of Rolls Royces,
but they fell into arrears on revenues.

When the rent collector arrived, they all
ran off, some by road, some by rail,
revealing no remorse. I had been
rejected. No one has rescued
me. Also, I am bored." And
she released a tear.

"Cheer up," said Ramsay
robustly. "Do not repine. Let's
explore the rectory!"

Ramsay, Rillah, and Ralph the red-nosed rat rambled all over the recently restored, romantic rectory. They reviewed the rotunda, which had a wide range of purloined reading materials; and the gallery, filled with fraudulent rococo artworks forged by professionals; and the cellar, with racks and racks of rare beverages ruthlessly plundered by Rillah's rascally relatives. At last they reached the rumpus room.

"This is the rumpus room," remarked Rillah regretfully, "but there has never been a rumpus in it. My relatives, though racketeers, were too refined for rumpuses. How I would relish regarding a real rumpus!"

"Your request is my resolve," replied Ramsay with a respectful gesture. "Return with me!"

So Ramsay, Rillah, and Ralph the red-nosed rat wriggled back through the Roman-vaulted rat-hole and reached the rectangular residence, where Ramsay's revolting relatives, Ron, Rollo, and Ruby, replete with rum, were relaxing in their recliners to the resounding rhythms of rock 'n' roll.

"Ready?" inquired Ramsay.

Rillah grinned in a refined but riotous manner.

"Rotten reindeer rinds reek, and so do Ron, Rollo, and Ruby!" Ramsay blared. "And your rock 'n' roll records are ridiculous!"

"Ramsay, you rabble-rouser! You are outrageous!" Ron, Rollo, and Ruby rose from their recliners like red-eyed rattlesnakes and went on the rampage. What a ruckus! Ramsay raced up to the roof garden, reversed direction, reeled through the root cellar, then ran round and round the revolving door, while his revolting relatives hurled ratchets, wrenches, wristwatches, radios, and rubber boots at his rear. But this time Ramsay ran so rapidly that they missed.

At last the revolting relatives ran out of steam and relapsed into a recumbent posture.

"Oh, Ramsay! That was a real rumpus!" trilled Rillah. "You may be rude, but you can run with a rapidity that erases boredom!"

"I would be less rude if I resided in the romantic rectory, surrounded by rhododendrons," replied Ramsay, "and could eat raspberries and rusks, instead of raw rhinoceros and rancid raisins."

"True," Rillah responded. "And I would be less tearful. To acquire a friend is refreshing, as well as reassuring."

"Do you like rats?" Ramsay queried, for it had occurred to him that the arrival of a new friend might cause Ralph to feel repudiated.

"There are few creatures I adore more than a rubicund, red-nosed rodent," Rillah replied, stroking Ralph's fur with terms of endearment. "Also, he will crunch up any roaches that may stray from the run-down side of the rampart."

"What about the rabid roaring radishes?" inquired Ramsay. "They regard me as a robber and will relentlessly rend me to shreds."

"They are not real radishes," replied Rillah. "They are robot replicas, cleverly arranged to repel intruders. I will reprogram them so they will be neutral in regard to you."

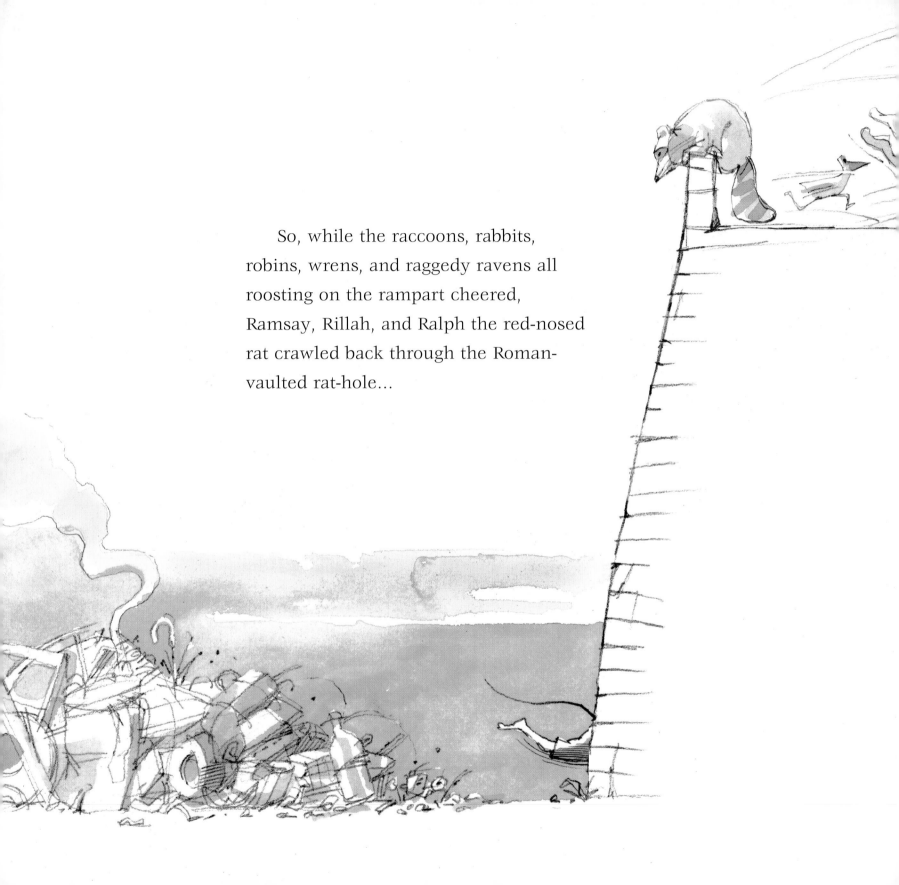

So, while the raccoons, rabbits, robins, wrens, and raggedy ravens all roosting on the rampart cheered, Ramsay, Rillah, and Ralph the red-nosed rat crawled back through the Roman-vaulted rat-hole...

...and romped rapturously among
the roses, beside the rippling river,
under the radiant rainbow.